# "RAINLIGHTS"

Written by: Claudine Darling

Illustrated by:  Cimi Pham

*This book is dedicated to one of the greatest gifts God ever gave me,
Hope, Faith and Love
To all the children at The Colonial Learning Center, Dallas Texas*

*"Believing in yourself when all odds are against you, is one of the
greatest virtues one can ever hope to have.*

Corey and his Scottie dog, Solo, walked into the forest. Corey could see the tall, green trees and berry bushes ahead of him. It was a warm, sunny day and the sun came shining through the tall forest trees as him and Solo walked along the path.

Corey had worn his favorite blue jean jacket. And inside his blue jean jacket was a small brown leather marble bag his Grandpa Cecil had given him last year for his birthday. He loved marbles and would collect them and put them in his brown marble bag which he carried with him.

Corey had several marbles, but only carried his three favorite, a yellow, a red and a green one. Last summer, Corey found a yellow marble lying in his backyard by an old oak tree. His Grandpa Cecil gave him a red marble for his birthday and he won the green marble playing marbles at school. Corey tucked his marbles in a leather bag in his jean jacket pocket.

Corey loved the forest. His dog Solo and he would walk in the forest every day after school. There was a little pond at the end of the path where Corey and Grandpa Cecil would go fishing. Corey collected rocks along the way.

When he reached the pond, he would throw rocks at the water, watching them skip and hop on top of the water.

Solo ran ahead of Corey, wagging his tail and sniffing all the little berry bushes along the path. "Solo! Solo!" Corey shouted. Corey could see Solo up ahead with his nose buried in a bush. Corey ran ahead to where Solo was and looked to see what solo was sniffing. Between the bushes a bright sparkling object appeared.

Corey picked it up and looked at it. It was a beautiful blue marble. Corey had never seen a blue marble like this one before. It was a large marble. About the size of a quarter and it sparkled with colors like a rainbow. He held it up in the air and looked into it and what appeared inside was a black eye, like a cat's eye.

Corey picked up another rock. He thought it was a rock, but he didn't know he had really picked up the yellow marble. Corey realized all his marbles fell out his jean jacket pocket. He threw the yellow marble across the pond. All of a sudden the pond turned into a yellow shiny marble floor. Corey closed his eyes and then opened them, but he still couldn't believe what he saw! The blue pond was gone!

Solo started barking and wagging his tail, running across the yellow marble floor. Corey quickly gather his marbles and put them back into his brown leather marble bag and tucked them in his jean jacket pocket. He closed his eyes again and stepped onto the yellow marble floor.

When Corey opened his eyes, he saw himself in the middle of the yellow, shiny marble floor. He walked around on it, still not believing his eyes. As he looked down on the yellow marble floor, there was his back yard and the old oak tree. There by the oak tree was the yellow marble he found last summer.

Corey bent down and tried to pick the yellow marble up. As he did, he began to fall through the yellow marble floor. "Solo! Solo," Corey yelled. "Where are you, Solo?"

All around him, as he was falling, there was a black sky with bright yellow moons and bright silver sparkling stars. Corey tried to reach out and touch the moons and stars as he fell downward, but they were too far away.

Suddenly with a big thump, Corey landed on something soft. "Crunch!" Corey sat up and looked around him. He had fallen into a big pile of colored leaves. He sat there looking around. "Wow!" Corey said, as he soon realized he was in another forest with tall green trees and it was raining!

The raindrops looked like huge colored tear drops with the twinkling lights in them. Corey had never seen rain like this before. He sat there in awe watching the colored "Rainlights" falling down. They came falling, falling down all around him.

Corey smiled as they made big splashes of puddles, leaving colored drops of red, blue, orange, green, yellow and purple. As the raindrops fell from the sky, they rolled off Corey and onto the ground so he didn't get wet. All the trees and bushes were sparkling with colored leaves of yellow, blue, orange, green, purple and red.

Corey heard a rustling noise nearby. He turned around and saw a black tail sticking up out of the colored leaves. It was wagging back and forth. A little black head popped out. Black ears and black nose appeared and started twitching back and forth.

Then it moved toward him. Corey jumped up! His eyes got big as he slowly backed away. It moved again!

"Solo," Corey cried, as Solo jumped out of the leaves and ran towards Corey. Corey bent down and scooped Solo into his arms and held him tight. Solo licked Corey's face all over. Corey laughed aloud, spinning Solo around in his arms.

Corey gently put Solo down and looked around the forest. He saw a sign that read, "Rainlight Village" with an arrow pointing down a path. "Hmmm," Corey thought, I wonder who lives, there?"

Corey started to walk along the path to "Rainlight Village."  Solo followed behind him.  Huge colored raindrops were still falling all round him and Solo.

He looked up at the trees.  They were twinkling with so many bright beautiful colors; yellow, orange, red, purple, green, blue.  "What an awesome forest," Corey said aloud.  "Grandpa Cecil would really love this forest."

Corey stopped and looked up into the trees.  He thought he heard a strange noise.  He listened carefully again, but he didn't hear anything.  He quickly began to walk again along the path.

All of a sudden, something jumped down from a tree in front of him. It began to run around and around Corey and Solo making a funny noise. "Eeeeeeeooooo, eeeeeooo, eeeeeeooo."

Solo began to bark. Corey quickly picked Solo up and stood still, afraid to move.

The creature slowed down and stopped in front of Corey. Corey didn't know what to do, run or stand still. It looked like a small color-spotted raccoon with big blue eyes and big bushy purple tail. It began to sniff Corey's tennis shoes. Corey could feel Solo shaking and tried to hold Solo tight against him.

The creature stopped sniffing, turned, and ran hurriedly down the path.

10

Solo leaped from Corey's arms and began to run after the strange-looking animal. Corey took off running after them.

Nearly out of breath, Corey reached a long red wooden bridge and saw the little creature still scurrying along with Solo running after it. In front of the old wooden bridge was a wooden sign that read "Rainlight Village."

Corey hurried to catch up with Solo. Before he got to the end of the bridge, his foot got caught between two boards. Corey reached for a rope that was along the side of the bridge and hung on tight. He tried hard not to look down at the water below.

A wind began to pick up and the bridge began to rock back and forth. Corey tried to get his foot loose.

The brown marble bag began to fall from his jacket. Corey took one of his hands off the rope and grabbed the marble bag and put it between his teeth. The green marble fell out. As the green marble fell towards the water, Corey lost his grip on the rope and began to fall too.

When the green marble hit the water, it created a giant green lily pad that Corey landed on. The lily pad floated to the other side of the water and Corey jumped off and climbed up the grassy hill.

Corey sat there for a moment. All Corey could think about was finding Solo. Corey got up and looked around. He could see ahead of him a little village with little stone huts. As Corey ran towards the village, he saw that the stone huts were old looking with brown straw roofs that had holes in them. The doors on the huts were gone and some of the windows were broken. There was no color anywhere. It was just a plain, muddy, brown, ugly village.

Corey felt sad. The village wasn't taken care of. It needed lots of work. Corey walked to the middle of the village.

There was a big dirt circle and in the middle of the circle was an old large gray stone that had writing on it. Corey read the writing on the large gray stone aloud.

"We are the Zamwas. We came here a long time ago. We built our huts of stone and straw with our hands and when the rain came, the village was filled with beautiful colors"

"This is why we call our village, "Rainlight Village." A long time ago, we lost a beautiful large blue round glass stone and that is when the twinkling colored raindrops stopped coming down. This is why our village has no color and has turned to mud and is ugly."

We are the Zamwas.
We came here a long time ago.
We built our huts of stone and straw
with our hands and when the rain came,
the village was filled with beautiful colors".
This is why we call our village
"Rainlight Village."

A long time ago, we lost a beautiful
large blue round glass stone,
and that is when
the twinkling colored raindrops
stopped coming down.

This is why
our village has no color
and has turned to mud and is ugly.

Corey remembered the large blue marble with the cat's eye he found and wondered if it was the precious stone that belonged to the Zamwas. He reached into his jacket and pulled his brown leather bag out and took the large blue marble out and laid it in the dirt circle. The large big blue marble with the cat's eye began to sparkle with a brilliant blue light and then it began to roll around Corey.

Corey watched the large blue marble dance around him. The wind began to blow. He could see eyes watching him behind the muddy ugly stone huts. The animal creatures began to appear from behind the stone huts. Corey held his jacket tighter around him and called for Solo. "Solo, Solo!" "Where are you, Solo?" he yelled.

The large blue sparkling marble began to make a sound. It was the sound he heard in the forest the little creature made, "eeeeeeeeeeeeooooo, "eeeeeeeeooooo."

In the middle of the circle a blinding white light appeared. In the white light stood a taller creature, like the little ones who was coming towards him. This creature had long white hair and wore a long blue robe with yellow moons and silver stars with a gold rope belt. His eyes were big and they sparkled like the large blue marble.

Within the illustration:

We are the Zamwas.
We came here a long time ago.
We built our huts of stone and straw
with our hands and when the rain came,
the village was filled with beautiful colors.
This is why we call our village
"Rainlight Village."

A long time ago, we lost a beautiful
large blue round glass stone
and that is when
the twinkling colored raindrop
stopped

This is
our village ha
and has turned to

Corey knew it was a "Zamwa" because the stone read "We are the Zamwas." The old Zamwa stood there holding a black cane in one hand and Solo in the other. Corey gently bent down and picked up the sparkling large blue marble.

Corey held his head down looking at the dirt holding the large blue marble close to him. He loved the big bright blue sparkling marble with the cat's eye that Solo found for him. But Corey knew in his heart that this was the Zamwa's precious blue lost stone.

With tears springing to his eyes, Corey slowly looked up at the old Zamwa and then at Solo. He gently held the precious blue marble out in the palm of his hand towards the old Zamwa. The old Zamwa slowly walked towards Corey and took the sparkling blue marble from Corey's hand.

The old Zamwa bowed his head and handed Solo to Corey. Corey reached for Solo and held him close against his jean jacket for a long time. Corey thought about how much he loved Solo and never wanted to lose him.

Corey looked up into the old white-haired Zamwas's deep blue eyes and smiled. The old white- haired Zamwa smiled back. Then the old white-haired lifted the sparkling precious blue stone with both hands high unto the sky. The wind calmed down. The trees stopped moving and it began to rain. Beautiful raindrops. Raining, raining, raining. Falling down, all around. Falling, falling down.

As the raindrops fell all round, the little village began to sparkle with colored "Rainlights." The raindrops twinkled, falling down, painting beautiful colors on the stone huts windows, doors and straw roofs. Turning them all into beautiful colors. Purple, blue, green, pink, orange, yellow, red. All the colors of the rainbow and more.

Eyes appeared from behind the huts as little Zamwas came out from behind the stone huts. They all came together and joined hands making a big circle dancing around Corey and Solo.

Corey began to get dizzy. He remembered his brown marble bag and took it out of his jacket and looked inside. The red marble that Grandpa Cecil gave him was the only one left. Corey began to feel homesick. He took the red marble out of the brown marble bag and held it tightly.

Everything was getting blurry. His head began to hurt. He had to sit down. Corey closed his eyes. Holding Solo tight and dreaming of home, he whispered. "Grandpa."

He felt a warm tingling in the palm of his hand where he held the red marble. It was glowing red. Corey slowly opened his eyes and looked around him. He was sitting by the pond against an old yellow oak tree. He felt Solo lying still in his arms, sleeping.

He heard a voice calling him, "Corey, Corey, where are you?" Corey knew the voice now. Corey quickly jumped up! Solo jumped out of Corey's arms and started running.

Grandpa!" Grandpa!" Corey yelled as he ran down the path home. He ran up to him and put his arms around him and hugged him. "Let's go home Grandpa!" Corey said. Grandpa chuckled aloud, patted Corey's head as he reached for Corey's hand. Solo ran along ahead, sniffing all the berry bushes.

At home that night, Corey and Solo snuggled in bed. Corey lay there thinking about the walk in the forest. He watched the lightening flash outside his bedroom window and it began to rain.

As the raindrops began to fall against the window pane, Corey held the marble bag in his hand close to his heart. And as he heard the rain gently falling down, Corey slowly closed his eyes and dreamed. He dreamed of colored "Rainlights." Beautiful colored "Rainlights"… they were falling down all around him. "Rainlights, falling raindrops, colors of purple, red, green, orange, pink and yellow..falling….falling….

Eeeeeeeeeeeeeeeeeeeeeeoooooooooooo….Eeeeeeeeeeeeeeeeo

# THE END